See this guy in the truck?
He's got no idea what he's in for.
He's a transfer. New to the force. And this...

is the City of Lost Girls.

The other guys think you're catatonic. Means they think you're fucked up.
I don't think that. I think you're scared. So I just want to go back to the beginning. Can we do that?
Nah, we can't do that. 'Cause that shit's jodido.
That shit is what the Duchess calls-
Straight fucked up.

I love the Duchess curses. I love cursing.
Fucker.
QUIT IT.
My best friend Eyepatch and me, we're like Orphan girls here.
Duchess says we're all orphans. Says she'll tolerate Eyepatch but reminds me-
We got too many scared women up here to worry about the past, Analia. We ain't got time for that. Nostalgia is a fucking assassin. You hear me?
'Cause far off in the heat are monsters.

They been hunting you since you were 14. Been smelling you since you were even younger.
See, your ass is MEAT.
And that shit's good. 'Cause meat is a lure. Meat is what makes these motherfuckers show themselves.

Motherfucker isn't something
I was allowed to say at home.

Analia, mantente alejado de la ventana.

I just want to look.
Dije que no.

Can't just keep us inside, Mama.
Who says?

No seas una perra
AYUDAME DIOS

Tonight, we paint the town Red. Screw Mama!

See every woman in here? They're all living! They aren't scared of what happens out there. They aren't scared of disappearing. 'Cause once they have your fear they own you. You gotta live, Analia.
I will.
Come on, I want to hear you.
I WILL!
Hell yeah, sodas for everyone.
We gotta fight but we don't gotta be scared, that's the point.
I won't be scared.
Look at you. My little badass!

But I wasn't a badass then.
Run.
Maria...
Mom? You gotta be badass. You gotta be-

Mama!
Help!
We gotta barricade the doors, Mama.
Que
Maria, Mama. They got Maria!
DONDE ESTA EL NEGRO

Duele! Matame!
She wants me to kill her, to save her from the pain.
I figure my life is over.
I'll take us all down.
Analia! Jump!
Valeria. She sits next to me in school and I ignore her because of her stupid hat.
I pretend...
I do not see her.
I'll protect you, Valeria. We'll be sisters. I promise...
...No one will ever hurt you again.

Valeria's parents ignored her too. They didn't even know she was gone. She said it was better. The abandoned train station is where we live now.
What's up?
I'm really sorry for everything.
BLVD ZARAGOZ
You don't have to apologize to me. You're special, Analia. I'm your best friend. You know I can see that.
I often think the two of us could escape this place, we could go off and be girls somewhere. Eyepatch thinks-
Even the Duchess says it- you're a bad bitch!
Sometimes I wonder if the two of us should just run away. But one thing keeps me-

You wanna pay back that sister blood, don't you Red? I ain't calling you Analia no more. Analia ain't what's gonna drip down your fingers.
Analia ain't what you learning about watching them samurai on TV.
Listening to doo-wop tapes while you fuck up the tumbleweeds.
It's gonna be Red.
And you're gonna be covered in it. I see it. Your sister would be a proud motherfucker!

Dolly Parton with those arrows.
Beyoncé with the darts.
And when you run? A fuckin' iron woman. I see a whole pack of coyotes gonna collapse before you let them four-legged freaks outrun you.
I know you don't want to be here. Don't like how we Victorias live. But you want your sister. You want revenge. And thing about humans, we are relentless motherfuckers. We won't stop. These coyotes keep hunting us but we won't hide. We won't cower.
Nah, Victorias fight. And we got a champion now. On a string, baby. We gonna do this together. We gonna-

Celebrate!!!

They call this COMING OUT NIGHT.

All the Victorias have one.
You must kill a COYOTE.
You must get its head.

Which brings us back to the actual beginning, I suppose.
I got a girl in here. Fuckin' traumatized. At least 20 bodies. Lots of women and children.
23 bodies.
8 kids. 10 women.
And me. Making paper cranes.
Mama, we'll be safe though?
Si. Up North they have all nice things. I can work at night and no one bothers me. We just have to get there.
Nothing can stop us, eh Mom?
Psst
Hey!
WHEN they COME RUN?
When who comes?
These.
Whatever, freak!

And they come
We're going to die, Momma.
Si, Mancho, si.
They didn't stand a chance.
The Duchess tells us the coyotes have been hunting us forever.
They are our neighbors. They are our friends.

The fur is just
a costume.

The teeth, some mystical bling.

But still...
Your sister
Maria Soto?

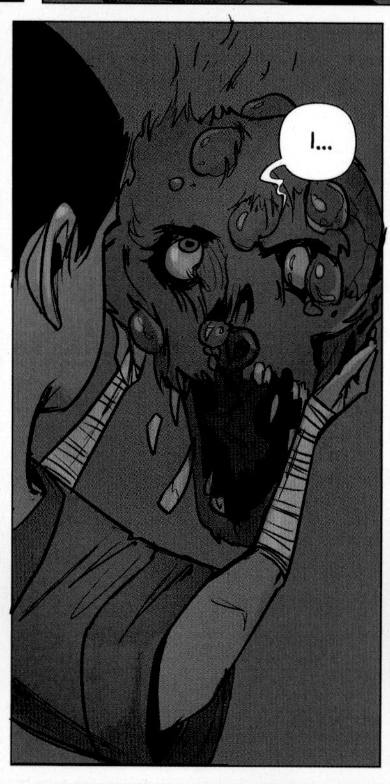
I...

Was her
busboy.

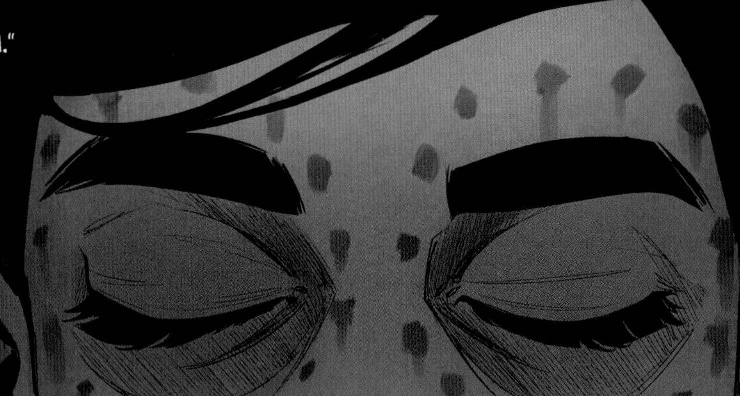
"When you find the coyotes, take their pelts."
"Why Duchess?"
"It's what makes these limp dicks transform into what they really are.
It gives these cowards teeth and fur."
"And my sister?"
"I'll tell you everything that happened."
"When?"
"When you bring me the pelts, little
bitch. When we burn that shit."
"I don't know, Duchess."
"There's nothing to know, baby.
Just close your eyes...
Remember, you'll always
be safe with us."

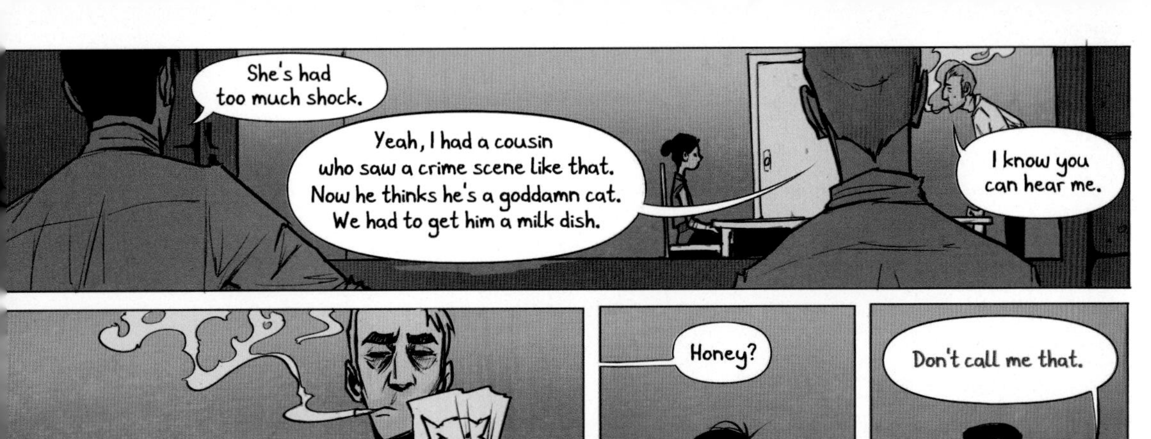

I think that will be enough! Yuki?

Are you okay?

What the hell are you doing?
Stopping the illegal questioning of a minor.
Pardonnez-moi

A French speaker. Oh hell no. That's not kicking my ass-

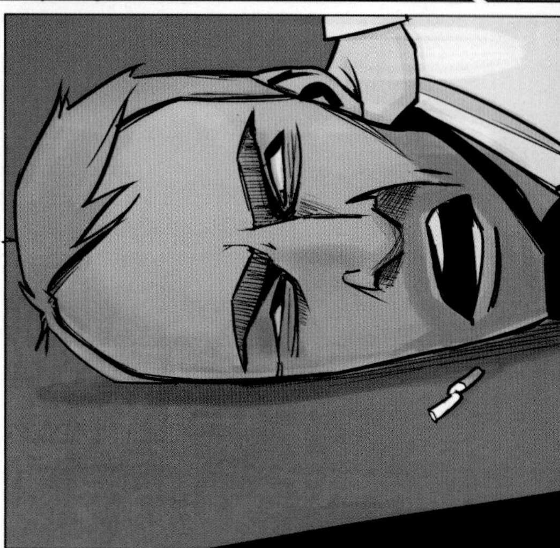

UGH

I'm a police officer, you can't just do that-

Welcome to the City of Lost Girls, transfer. You stop letting our bodies end up in ditches and we'll stop pissing on your badge. Good day!

THEY ARE REAL-ANALIA
Why did I warn him?
I guess he seemed dumb and innocent like the boy on the truck.
And I've seen enough people die.
'R'RRRING'
Real?
Boss, I don't think you're gonna believe this.

But we got something you're gonna need to see.
WELCOME TO THE
CITY OF LOST GIRLS

Simple formula. You do the right thing.

You study. You work hard.
You serve the community.

You don't be an asshole.

"COFFEY"

You need to come home, Frank.
BEEEEEEEP
After I finish this job.
This is your family-
Stacey, I have a job-
SMASH
Everyone's an asshole.
If you don't come home now, your daughter and I won't be here when you finally decide to
Fuck, I forgot to hang up.
Frank?
I gotta go.

Fuckin' girl is the same age as my daughter.
And the mom...Christ...
Fuckin' truck driver hands me a business card– ADLIN INDUSTRIES– he might as well say "this is my get-out-of-jail-free card."
ADLIN owns everything.
ADLIN is untouchable.
When you're a dad, you see a little kid hurting and you think, "What if that was my kid?"
And that makes no one untouchable.
I'm not untouchable. This job made me a shitty dad. Shittier husband. Serve the community, right?

See my wife leaving with my daughter? See the house keys left with the family photos?
See what I made of myself after 13 years on the force. How's that for service?
What the fuck are you bringing an ADLIN guy in for?
He killed a girl's mom.
They're already taking the cuffs off the ADLIN asshole.
Get out of jail free, you see.

Look, you're getting transferred.
You care about this muck work then you're gonna get a lot of it.
What?
Transferred? What the fuck are you talking about?
City of Lost Girls. Hope it doesn't piss your wife off.
Yeah, you'll get to see a lot worse than fucking crashed cars out there.
No hard feelings. We need dedicated cops out there.
Yeah, because we all know dedication doesn't do shit.

I dedicated my life to upholding the law.

How stupid, after all, what the fuck is the law?

I call my wife.

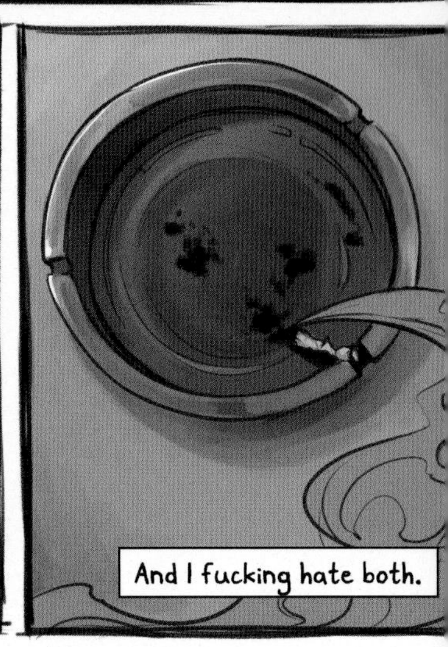

Traditionally, there were several ways that a person could become a werewolf. In her book *Giants, Monsters, and Dragons*, folklorist Carol Rose said, "In ancient Greece it was believed that a person could be transformed by eating the meat of a wolf that had been mixed with that of a human and that the condition was irreversible." Centuries later other methods were said to create werewolves, including, "being cursed, or by being conceived under a full moon, or by having eaten certain herbs, or by sleeping under the full moon on a Friday, or by drinking water that has been touched by a wolf."
It was also widely believed that werewolves could dress in a special, protective wolf skin, though they had to remove it at daybreak and hide it. If their magical pelt was found and taken from the werewolf while in human form, he or she could be killed.
I don't need the whole history.
Just the precedents. In 1589, a German named Peter Stubbe claimed to own a belt of wolfskin that allowed him to change into a wolf. His body would bend into a lycan form, his teeth would multiply in his mouth, and he craved human blood.

Stubbe claimed to have killed at least a dozen people over 25 years- though his confession was made under difficult circumstances.

Difficult, how?
Well, someone set him on fire, so we can't be sure if he was telling the truth or not.

GNA...

Holy shit, the motherfucker speaks.
My friend, what was that?

NOT MY FRIEND

Are we-?

We are fine.
Poor thing, really.
Get the window fixed and keep shearing him. The pelts made from his skin have worked well on the men in town. They've really taken to hunting. The beast is a godsend, let's keep getting what we can from him.
GAIA, MY LORD.
I WILL FIND HER.

You sure this empty shithole is the place? Why the fuck would girls live in a train station? Must smell like piss and homeless in there. Not even an address.
We asked around, boss. Bunch of women dressed in old British lady shit is hard to miss.
Fine. Keep an eye out. When I see her, I'm going in.
Tell me, what was it like? Come on?
No, you're it. If you catch me, maybe!

The Duchess says it's important to celebrate every night so the monsters see we have no fear. No fear of men who try to hunt us in pelts. No fear of "coyotes." We don't respect them enough to call them wolves, the men. They are weak and hunt in packs.

No fear of a much more ancient force that w
know is in the wind. A large howl that's called f
women like us, forever. Those are the real wol
Those are the enemies we one day will war wit

If we ever stop dancing. Playing. Living. They hate to see us living.

Red?
You know we aren't supposed to be near the Duchess' quarters.
This is some off-limits hide-and-go-seek, yo!
Deja de intentar assustarme!
Bitch! What are you doing in here? Scared me to death, ha!
Valeria, would you leave with me?

Leave? Why?
If the Duchess lied to us. A coyote last night, he said something about her and my sister-
The Duchess has protected us.
But if we found out there was something she kept from us?
We should go, come on.
You remember Maria, my sister? Well, why does the Duchess have this?
What are you doing in Duchess'car?

You think you are hot shit because of last night, Red. The Duchess saw you leave the party. She sends Catalina.
And Catalina-
...fucks you up!
Ugh! Hate you-
NEVER TOUCH HER!!!
Like the Duchess says, it just comes out of me. The Hurt. And when it does, I'm dangerous.

People always want to help people who seem hurt.
Seems stupid to me.
Hello, I'm looking for the young woman I met at yesterday's crime scene? If I'm lucky, she doesn't think she's a cat at this point?
Duchess thinks it comes from man's inherent need to help.
I'm a police officer and though you might not find that cool, I'm here to help.
DO NOT ENTER
I think we should've ignored it when we evolved. Help means you're weak. Help means you couldn't do it yourself.
OH SHIT.
HALT!!!

That's right!
Respect the law!
Um, when the fuck
did wolves start talking?
This is new, right?
FOLLOWED
YOUR
SCENT
BAD
WOMEN
TAKEN

They aren't wolves, just stupid coyotes- my doll!

TROUBLE TROUBLE

Let's get back to the point- I don't know why the Duchess has a doll of my sister.

But fuck if I'll let some fucking "coyotes" take it.

You two ready?

Catalina is ready. Catalina is a bad motherfucker.

Hear me you fucking coyotes!

Me too. Coffey is also a bad motherfucker. Thank you.

Women always have been at the front of revolution.
What the fuck!
Seriously?
I was playing odds Catalina would dodge.
Cause women know a liar when they see one. They know violence on the horizon. You have to when you got little chiquitas in your belly.
Basically,

women sound the alarm!
Someone called?
Last time I saw these assholes, I lost a brother.
A husband.
I been waiting for this.
Mantalos?
Oh hell yeah. A whole fucking lot of Mantalos!
VICTORIAS

We took our name from the queen the train station was named for.
I don't think she fought werewolves (though who knows, England is all sorts of fucked up).
But I bet she took what she wanted.
You, take my hand!
I'm supposed to be leading you out.
Really? I thought you wanted to survive...

I was so angry and lost when I met the Duchess. I wanted to be around other women so badly, mothers and sisters-

I think I shit myself. Those wolves, you called coyotes. You drew them at the station-

HEY. I don't need gross details on your pants!

But dolls like this? I need you to tell me: Where would I get these?

Fuck.

I think I actually know.

Duchess, Catalina!
Where?
With the coyote. He's transforming.
She got bit.
Catalina saw Red find her sister's doll. She'll go to the old woman. Catalina tried-
Stop
You can hear me in your head Catalina.
You have to give in. You were very brave.
But this will make it go faster.
And Red-
Red we will deal with.
Bury them and get armed.

Dolls look real, right? We call this Creepsville.

Valeria will be mad I left her behind, but she doesn't need to see this.

What is this place?
Not sure. A woman lost a daughter and swore she saw her up here. Turned out that it was just a doll. All these dolls are missing people.

Who makes them?
We weren't sure,
but, oh shit-
I think we're about
to find out.

I am ABUELA.

"DUCHESS"

You have a girl in your town people talk shit about?
"She's fast."
"She's wild."
When I was young, I was different.
When I was young...

...that girl was me.
Faster!
Don't worry, when we stop, the three of us are gonna go real fast, mi amor.
Only if you stop saying that mi amor shit.
I told you she'd be up for this.
If we had sex, fine. If we got drunk, even better.
As long as we did something.
"Girls you better watch out, Some boys are only about, That thing, that thing-"
Ready?
You look ridiculous. Are those pelts?
I learned the hard way.
Fangs. Claws.
This wasn't sex.
This wasn't fun.
This shit was track.

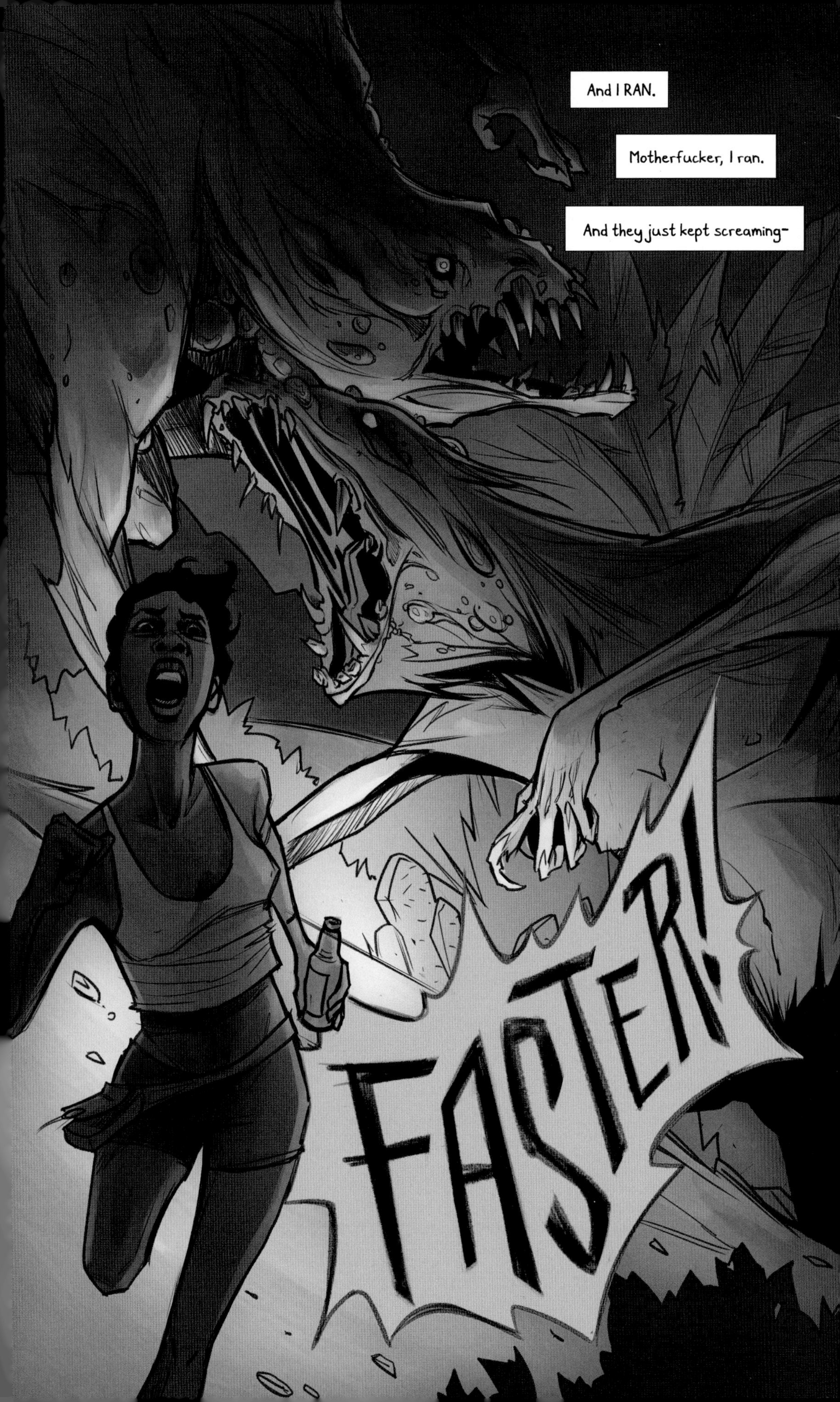
And I RAN.
Motherfucker, I ran.
And they just kept screaming-
FASTER!

PUTA
Get off me.
Fuck you.
Drown in your own blood, bendejo.
Cause you ain't getting me.
WRONG MI AMOR
Wha?
ACCKGH

I'm Maria.
She was the girl who ran the diner in town.
She took me to Victoria Station.
You should be proud. Not a lot of women take out a coyote with their bare hands.
Proud? I almost got killed because I was gonna let those guys do whatever with me tonight.
You're not alone. You'll come to my house. Stay in my room with me and my sister. OK?
"OK." But when we got there...

I saw her younger sister. She was too young.
Too innocent.
I was too wild for her sphere.
I was ashamed. Girl who met two dudes behind a bar and ended up like this.
So, I left.
Years later when that girl would meet me again, she wouldn't even remember.
I went back to Victoria Station.
And it was like they were waiting for me.
Who are you?
We are your future. Now it's time to kick some ass.
And all praise, a Duchess was born.

You bring a man here?
No male shall survive this dwelling.
ACKKGH
Who knows. Little girls might die, too.

After all, in the old days we had respect. Understand?
It's tough with all that old person breath.
Just my own death coming, little one. And your death?
Isn't gonna be by some damn grandma. Coffey?
Working on it. It's fire, you know!
But don't worry. I'm an officer of the law.
I get shit done!

Where's my sister?
You make the dolls!
Where is she?
Fuck this niñita.
Bring a man into my house.
Desecrate my dolls.

Now
I'm ready
to talk.

Abuela? Come out.
They are with me.

You know what we agreed.
You have your way and I have mine.
I didn't send her.
She came on her own. I swear.
She brought that thing-

"Man." She brought that man. Jesus Christ. You shot at me and set me on fire. Give me at least my fucking gender!

She found this.

Ah, Maria. We blessed her with charm. Not that she needed us to.

You blessed her? Who the fuck are you? Why was that in your room, Duchess?
She's my sister, who the fuck are you?

Abuela is a Grandmother of the Desert. A Daughter of Gaia.

I am dying.
We all are-

I see my Sisters heard the ruckus.

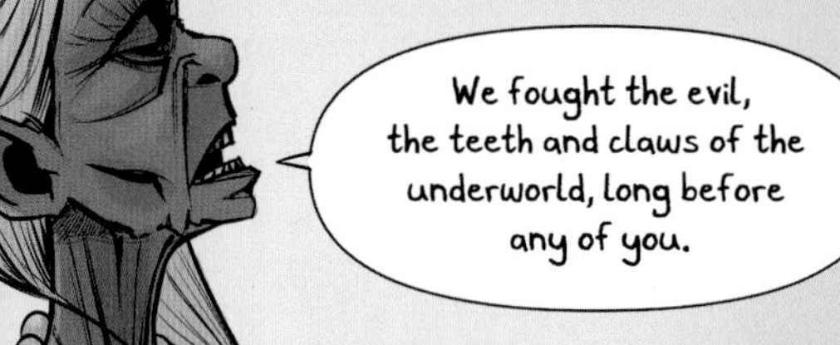
We fought the evil, the teeth and claws of the underworld, long before any of you.

Centuries.

But now we are dying away.

So they entrusted me to find more. Ones they could bless.
My sister?
Maria built morale. It's why they killed her.

And me?

You - if you're willing, Red - you are blessed to be our champion.

It's earlier than we wanted it to happen. Earlier than it should. You may not be ready. But there is no more waiting.

This is nuts. You're all fucking nuts.

Are we? Know a lot of grandmothers who jump off walls?

It's what you want. Be brave.

What is next?
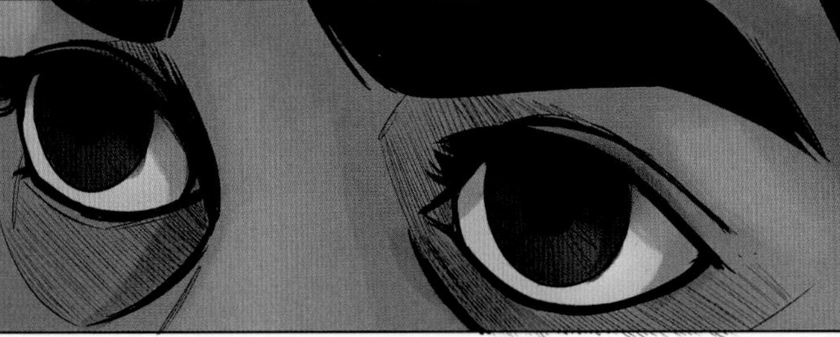

Adlin.
Adlin? The weapons builder? What do they have to do with this?

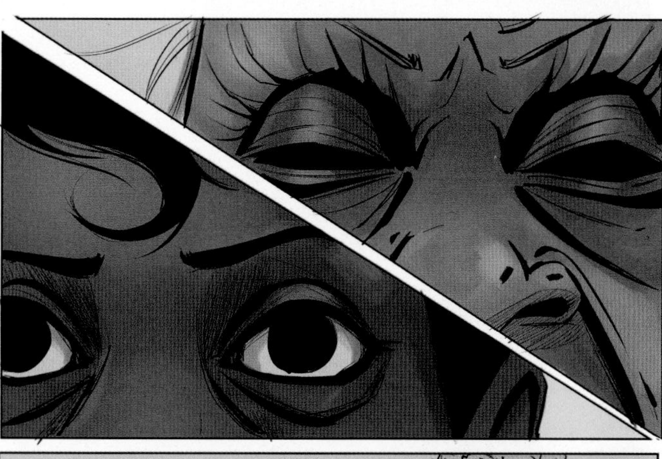

You're sure now?

I've been watching them for weeks, and if there is a wolf from the ancient times, it is there and it is being used.
So we fight our way through.

Unless you don't have to. Such a smart leader, I'm surprised. Never heard of a bait and switch?

Coffey's the bait.

I need to know
the story in case I am
missing something.

I WILL EAT YOUR FACE. I WILL DEVOUR THE ONE BEHIND YOU-

Now, now - we brought you outside for some sun. This is nice, isn't it?

There were Wolves first. Along with dinosaurs, reptiles, sea animals-
WE WERE IN THE WOODS, WE HUNTED ALONE
And then what-

A GREAT FLAME FROM THE SKY.
A meteor. And this is when you say there were no more dinosaurs?

THERE WAS NO MORE ANYTHING.
WE ROAMED THE WOODS WITH NO PLANTS, TREES ALL NAKED, NO ANIMALS-
How did you survive?
WILL. ROTHSCHILD. WILL.
Yes. And then-

WE SAW GREEN. WE SAW FLOWERS. WE SAW LIGHT.
GAIA.
Where did she come from?
SHE SPRANG FROM THE DIRT. SHE EMERGED FROM THE TREES.

GODDAMMIT.
I need facts, SEFF. I need usefulness. She sprang out of the dirt?
WHERE DID THE ANCIENT WOLVES COME FROM? SHE INVITED US IN. BUT WE ARE WOLVES.

JUST LIKE THE MEN YOU GIVE MY HAIR TO.

MEN YOU FEED MY MEAT TO.

We use inmates because no one asks questions about them. It is the same reason we have the victims of our tests-

THE WOMEN.

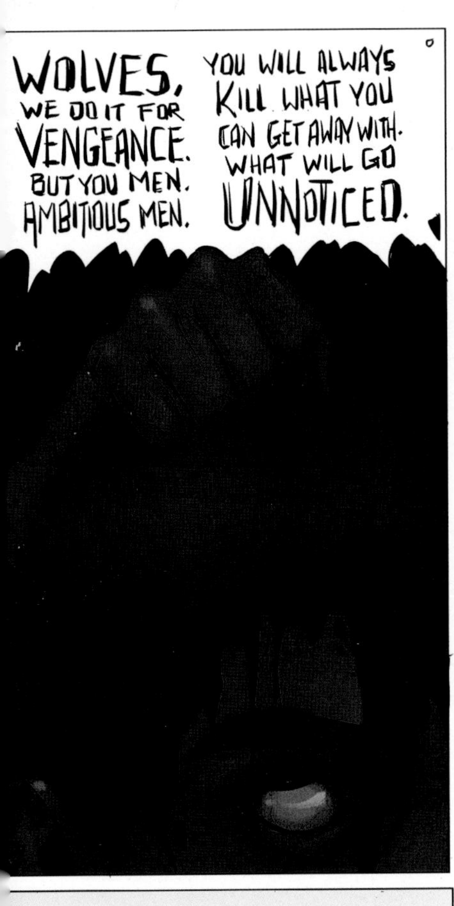
WOLVES, WE DO IT FOR VENGEANCE. BUT YOU MEN. AMBITIOUS MEN.
YOU WILL ALWAYS KILL WHAT YOU CAN GET AWAY WITH. WHAT WILL GO UNNOTICED.

THIS IS WHY WE WERE TOSSED OUT. IT WAS OUR NATURE. IT IS YOURS TOO. NOT JUST BECAUSE THE MEN YOU PICK ARE BAD. BUT BECAUSE IT IS SIMPLY WHO YOU ARE.
Interesting. Carl, I want to test the genetics of the fur. Perhaps the men are taking on his vengeance.

He said we're evil.
Maybe we are, Carl. I think there's a test you can help us with too.

Once you've changed your pants.

Mr. Sampson, you have a guest?
What are you talking about?
Me.
Detective Coffey.
This little man is talking about me.
Leave us.

Do you have it?
The camera will be on a loop.

Go in, find the man Red knows and take out as much of the interior as you can.
What about you?

CLICK
CLICK
We'll find the wolf. You kill the men.

Will do.
You ready?
I'll try to be.
You will be.

I wasn't looking for a track meet. I had a few questions. You employ a lot-
The Better to EAT YOU WITH!
Ex-cons. You're a cop. Don't be squeamish.
Yes. And, well, we got a disappearing woman problem in this city-
SSSSSSSSS
Yes-

What the fuck is this?

Sorry, boss. We had to let the other boss know. You were actually on to something.

Rashom? Toots?

It must've worked. There's no security at all.
Wait.
No security, that isn't right. Even with the loop-
Oh fuck.

DUCK!
We got to hide. There's so many of them.
I think it's too late.

Stand behind me.
Jesus Christ, where is the Duchess?

VALERIAAAA!!!!!!!!!
She is my best friend. She would've run away with me if I wanted. But I needed this and so she needed it too. Will everything be destroyed so I can get some closure? Will I do that to those who are close to me? I can't...I won't...
Valeria! I'm sorry!
Just finish it.
Just do that!

IT'S BEEN A LONG TIME.
They mirrored a spell with their science. It's why he can't break through it even though it's fragile.
STILL RECRUITING?
We've come to kill you.
FINALLY.
You're resigned?
THIS ISN'T MY WORLD ANYMORE.
Perhaps you're right.
Duchess.
No, for now... for now, there ar greater evils in the world.
DUCHES

TO FIGHT IS ONE THING,
BUT TO ENSLAVE!!!!!!!!

"Science does not care if you are a good person."

"ROTHSCHILD & SAMPSON"

Science only cares about more science.
Tell me your trepidation?
We're a weapons manufacturer.
What better weapon than people themselves?
You are talking about werewolves.
Yes.
I don't have time for fairy tales and myths, Dr. Rothschild.
Bring me Marcos.

Hello, Marcos.
I have a pelt for you.
H-hi.
Can I put it on my bear?
No. Just for you.
O-okay.
What is with the kid?
Your company, Adlin Enterprises, has existed for the better part of 200 years. You were started in the shadows. World War I. World War II. Korea. Vietnam. Iraq.
Every advancement in technology that killed people, you have been at the beginning of it.
Where did you find this boy, Rothschild?
The desert, looking for his brother.
You're making a biological weapon?
Of a sort. We're making people into weapons.

BROTHER!!! RAMON!!! BROTHER!!!
Oh my god.
This desert houses a wolf. His hair makes the pelts that make the monsters.

There's too many of them.
They're too strong.
NEED A MIRACLE, LITTLE GIRL.

ALL THEY NEED IS SEFF
YOU LOOK LIKE WOLVES BUT NOT MOVE LIKE A REAL WOLF NOT VICIOUS LIKE AN ANCIENT WOLF NOT DESPERATE, ISOLATED, ALONE LIKE THE WORLD'S TRUE WOLVES

LITTLE BOYS
DRESSED LIKE LITTLE COYOTES.
CRACK
...epatch?!
My arm.
Oh my god.

I think...
I think this is the end of my story.
You're my family. I can't avenge my family and lose you.
RED...
The fucker's getting stronger.

SO THEY FOUND THEIR GIRL

NOW LET'S PLAY, LITTLE GIRL

She freed
the Ancient?
I told you
we should not
trust her again.
I told you Seff
would wreck shit for us
before he inevitably
turns on us.
Yes...
CRACK
What
do you say,
Duchess?
That I
trained the baddest
one among us. Don't
forget that! And
remember-

I'm a Vicious Bitch myself.
OOOFFFFFF
You are insolent. You will learn!
Grandma, please! All anyone needs to learn-

Is sticks are a bullshit weapon. Now listen up...

This is some next-wave feminism shit. Which means I'm the Queen Bitch and the rest of you better get with the Tide.
Now we got an animal to control.
Never liked her.
Enough. You heard her. Come.

ONCE THESE BOYS ARE DONE IT WILL BE YOU, ABUELAS.
The men are losing their pelts.
Ladies, I doubt I have to ask-

ABUELAS
Let's fuck some shit up.

We just want to go, we didn't sign up for this. They came and took us out of the prison and started dressing us, it wasn't our fault-
What's in your hand?
Please-
A trophy, huh?
What was her name?
Who?
The hair?
Amanda. I'm sorry, thank you for sparing me.
I'm not sparing you.
What?
I'm making you easier to smell.
Smell-

KILL THEM ALL
SEFF!!
We are not your friends and WE WILL SETTLE THIS. But not today. You were chained.
You were prey.
Unsafe.
Hunted.
Us.

We live like that every day. Fearful.
Hopeless.
I need to find the detective.
Looking for revenge.
You can die now or you can die later. The question is, do you want revenge on the people who chained you?
REVENGE ON THEM. REVENGE ON YOU. ON YOUR MOTHER AND YOUR SISTERS
Don't make us kill you now-

LADIES.
Let's step away from my property.
Seff, we've been such a good team. Be a good pet and roll over.
Hello?

Coffey!
Run, kid!
Oh, I like little girls. Here, kitty kitty.
Don't call me a cat-
Unless you want your balls on a string.
I'm gonna throw up.
Let me help.
Christ!

Let me the fuck out of here.
Funny when monsters lose their power-
They don't really want to fight.
They just want to run.
Like a stuck pig. All these pictures of girls on these walls. All these lives you stole.
You don't deserve it to be this easy.
You don't need to say anything.
Red...

Just look.
This is what people do to us. They make us pose. And then they make us disappear.
No, Red!
I can't believe a fucking child created this much trouble.
Motherfucker.
Choke you to death-

Hole in my chest. On that wall with those women.
I am those women. We're blood. We're red.
Make me live in a world with men like you.
BAA
AAGGHHHH
For my daughter. For that girl I saw back home. For all of 'em, asshole.
Is this evidence?
Doesn't matter.
Red!
I got you.
Besides, shit this vile, you just gotta burn it all down.

When the smoke clears, you'll all know who's in charge. Ok, pretty faces?
No one else needs to get hurt.
What the fuck is this?
Now, I will be leaving with my property. Seff, come along.
AAGGH

Motherfucker thinks he can just blow my face off.
Look at me.
I suppose you have something poetic to say-
Not really.
BOOM
You.
It was your fur that made these men into what they were? Made them terrorize all these women? My mom? My sister?
YES
Next time...

No more.
He's going to kill her.
Wait.
ALK TO
ME LIKE
THAT, CHILD
YOU WILL NOT BE SPARED.
You don't understand. I'm the wolf now.
And I'm sparing you.
WE WILL MEET AGAIN, CHILD. AND I WON'T BE ALONE.

She fought bravely.
You should be proud of her.
I pray to the souls of great women
Women better than me
I pray to the stars of friends who have been lost
To a galaxy that burns bright to remind us we are not alone
Souls too bright to extinguish
I pray to the grandmothers
To clothe my friend
To feed her
To watch her
To know how missed she shall be
She is
And how sorely I let her down.
I owe her everything.

I'm sorry about your friend.
She gave her eye for me. Now she dies for me.
What are you doing?
No more dolls for missing girls. My friend comes back to the city. We aren't going to die in silence anymore. We aren't going to be silent. We aren't going to be unseen.
I told you.
You did. Now we have our champion.

"For the women lost I am there.
For the women frightened I am watching.
And I will fight with you."

"THE FUTURE"
RRAWR
What is it?
Hush.
Momma.
Run.
What is it?
It's the only way to get away from the monsters here.
You have to ride a monster north.
The Beast.

Look at this idiot.
Not nice, Grandma.
Come here, muchacho.
Thanks!
No problem, we needed something to eat for dinner.
Don't mind her.

I got my eyes on tastier meat.
Scumbag.
Is this yours?
I need help finding my brother. If you help me, I can give you this.
My mom gave one each to my brother Ramon and me.
Where is this Ramon?
I don't know.
I think the Beast will show me.
Grandma, what do you think?
SANCTUARY CITY 300 MILES
You aren't a wolf?
No.

I only trust rabbits.

That I promise.

And the blood?
It's so cute, right? Go Team!
POLICE DEPARTM
CITY OF LOST GIRL
352701

What were you girls doing?
Things you boys won't. Thank you. Idiot.
POLICE DEPARTMENT
CITY OF LOST GIRLS
352706

What's this one's deal?
She watched a lot of old movies with her grandma.
YOU FLAT FOOTS WILL NEVER TAKE ME ALIVE!!!
POLICE DEPARTMENT
CITY OF LOST GIRLS
352704

Um...?
I asked if she was ready for her picture to be taken.
POLIC
CITY
3
MENT
IRLS
0
....cheese...

Why would such a pretty girl be caught at such a grisly scene?
I guess I just have a bad home life. Asshole.
POLICE DEPARTMENT
CITY OF LOST GIR
352707

What do you got on her?
They said she was chewing on an animal bone when we arrived.
GODDAMN RIGHT I WAS. AREN'T YOU SUPPOSED TO HAVE DONUTS?
POLICE DEPARTMENT
CITY OF LOST GIRLS
352703

Name.
Duchess.
Though you can call me Your Highness. I got a feeling you should get used to it.
POLICE DEPARTMENT
TY OF LOST GIRL
352708

Should we bother?
Um, miss-
I ain't looking at anyone with that much coffee on their breath.
POLICE DEPARTMENT
CITY OF LOST GIRLS
352702

A completely wandering essay.

First. Thanks. From Caitlin and me. It's been amazing making this book. Sharing this book. Traveling to different cities and signing this book. We are over the moon.

Caitlin and I started working on this book over 2 years ago. I'd found her online. I sent a random email, "Hey I'm doing a comic at Image. I have no idea if they'll ever publish another one of mine. Want to try and make something together?" I sent her a short story. The story was about a girl with a katana blade killing werewolves. The story was COYOTES.

I don't know where this came from. I was thinking about coyotes who smuggle people across borders and the idea of borders, themselves. I was thinking about violence. I was thinking about my son. I was thinking about fairytales.

My writing process is to start with everything. All of it on the paper. All guts. All messy. And then I try, best as possible, to get rid of none of it. Instead, I try and figure out how it all COULD work together.

Caitlin, is obviously a superstar. It's nice to have an artist who makes me want to be a better writer. She makes trying things like this together so much easier, because, well, she makes those things look beautiful.

Comics are a hard business.

But neither of us would trade it, because sometimes you got to make this.